Googoo
and the
Morgantrains

C.S. Ryckman

WestBow Press books may be ordered through booksellers or by contacting:

WestBow Press
A Division of Thomas Nelson & Zondervan
1663 Liberty Drive
Bloomington, IN 47403
www.westbowpress.com
844-714-3454

Because of the dynamic nature of the Internet, any web addresses or links contained in this book may have changed since publication and may no longer be valid. The views expressed in this work are solely those of the author and do not necessarily reflect the views of the publisher, and the publisher hereby disclaims any responsibility for them.

Any people depicted in stock imagery provided by Getty Images are models, and such images are being used for illustrative purposes only.
Certain stock imagery © Getty Images.

ISBN: 979-8-3850-0428-7 (sc)
ISBN: 979-8-3850-0429-4 (hc)
ISBN: 979-8-3850-0430-0 (e)

Library of Congress Control Number: 2023914276

Print information available on the last page.

WestBow Press rev. date: 1/11/2024

WESTBOW
PRESS®
A DIVISION OF THOMAS NELSON
& ZONDERVAN

Googoo
and the
Morgantrains

Googoo Morgantrain is a fine boy. He has tiny feet and great big teeth and is the eldest son of his father Pete. Googoo's real name is Charles, but he is called Googoo because of the sound he liked to make as a baby.

Peter is a teacher and has fun being a daddy.

7

Googoo's mommy is Gail. She is a doctor and takes care of many people at the hospital. She sometimes wears a mask so she doesn't get sick at work.

Peter and Gail are both very tall.

11

The Morgantrains live in a brick house surrounded by big trees that are full of giant leaves.

Peter and Gail come from families with
lots of brothers and sisters and so
did their mommies and daddies.

15

Googoo has two younger brothers,
Mookie and Chaos.

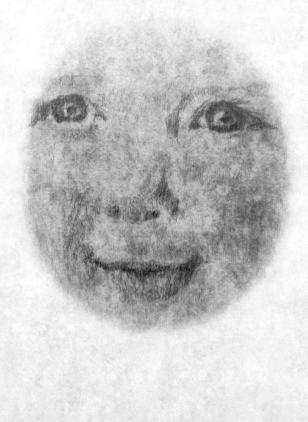

Mookie's name is Michael, but he's called Mookie because that is what Googoo calls him. Chaos is the youngest. His real name is Ernest, but his parents call him Chaos because they never know what he will do next.

19

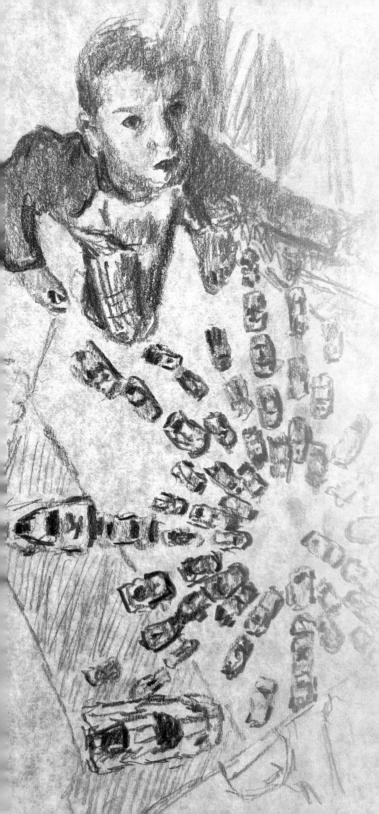

The boys love
dinosaurs and they
like to collect things,
especially rocks,
leaves, toy cars,
trucks and sea shells.

21

When people see the boys at play they often say, "Amazing!", because the boys are always moving, except when they're sleeping.

And when they sleep they dream
about adventures they want to have.
They all sleep in the same room.

Googoo and Mookie share a large bed. Chaos has his own bed because he moves around a lot. There are stars on the walls and ceiling, which shine from a lamp.

The boys like to play hide and seek and hide in small baskets and cardboard boxes.

They shoot basketballs
inside and outdoors.

And they make clubhouses to play in,
sometimes with Mommy and Daddy.

33

They race their cars on tracks
and wrestle every day.

37

Chaos has learned
many wrestling
tricks from Googoo
and Mookie.

Daddy taught the boys how to roller blade and he lets them race in the hallways of the house.

41

They play on the playground
in the backyard, which took
Daddy two days to build.

43

They play with Play-Doh and paint pictures at the kitchen table, where they also inspect sea shells.

46

They race each other on big wheels through the house and when they're tired they might look at books and read to each other--- even though they don't know how to read.

49

They like to play with blocks
and jump in the bouncy
house downstairs.

They argue over who gets to turn the bouncy house on and off because they like to see it get big and small.

They practice doing somersaults and headstands, and sometimes they try to make music on the piano. It gets a little noisy.

55

Googoo is really fast. He likes to bounce around on his toes and run as fast as he can and slide on his knees. Most of his pants have patches on the knees. His mommy sews them on. She is proud of how far he can slide.

57

The boys help around the house some.
Mookie has fun, even when he is cleaning,
because he thinks the vacuum cleaner
is a toy. And it has been one of his
favorite toys since he was really little.

It doesn't bother Chaos that he is the youngest of the boys, because he is a little giant. He is tall and very strong. He thinks he can do everything Googoo and Mookie can do.

61

Sometimes his brothers don't share toys, so Chaos carries his favorite toys around with him to always have something to play with.

Chaos often watches his brothers play and goes into another room so he can have all the toys in that room to himself.

65

Every room in the Morgantrain
house is a playroom.

They use mommy and daddy's bed for pillow fights and wrestling and they keep toys in the shower.

The garage doesn't have cars inside. It is filled with bicycles, scooters and other playthings.

The Morgantrains like to ride
bikes. Mommy and Daddy
built ramps and ride with
the boys around and round
in the driveway. Chaos is
too small to ride a bike so
he pushes anything he can
with wheels over the ramps.

The Morgantrains love to take long walks in the woods along creeks, and ride their bikes to play at the beach, which is on a big lake near their home.

They swim and throw rocks into the water
and sometimes watch the sun go down.

After they get home Mommy and Daddy fix dinner. When they are done eating the boys shower and sometimes watch a fun show. Because they are best friends they like to sit in a big chair together.

After this, they listen to a Bible story
to learn how to be good boys and
then they go upstairs to bed.

They say their prayers and are tucked into bed. The lamp with the stars is turned on. Peter and Gail watch and listen to the boys from the family room downstairs. The boys like telling stories to each other so Peter and Gail have to tell them to "Stop talking and go to sleep."

83

When things get quiet, Peter and Gail
give each other a big hug and say,

AH!

and...

Thank you
GOD
for another
beautiful
DAY

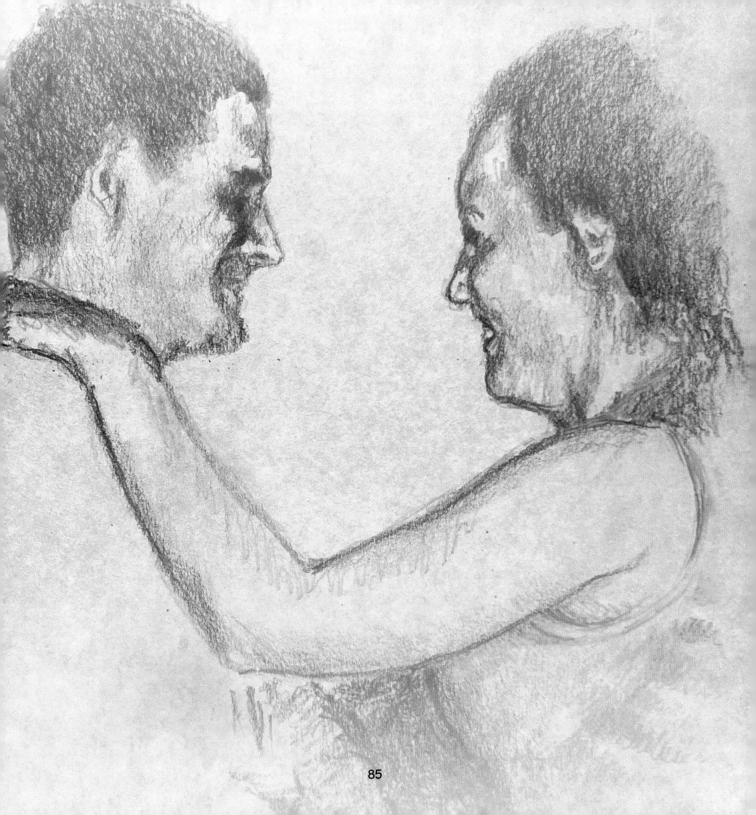

Special thanks to my wife, Therese, and the members of the Matty Adkins family.

Bye, Bye.

Printed in the United States
by Baker & Taylor Publisher Services